Bunny Needs a Friend

The Royal Society for the Prevention of Cruelty to Animals is the UK's largest animal charity. They rescue, look after and rehome hundreds of thousands of animals each year in England and Wales. They also offer advice on caring for all animals and campaign to change laws that will protect them. Their work relies on your support, and buying this book helps them save animals' lives.

www.rspca.org.uk

Bunny Needs a Friend

By Jill Hucklesby
Illustrated by Jon Davis

SCHOLASTIC

First published in the UK in 2014 by Scholastic Children's Books
An imprint of Scholastic Ltd
Euston House, 24 Eversholt Street
London, NW1 1DB, UK
Registered office: Westfield Road, Southam, Warwickshire, CV47 0RA
SCHOLASTIC and associated logos are trademarks
and/or registered trademarks of Scholastic Inc.

ISBN 978 1407 13965 4

A CIP catalogue record for this book is available
from the British Library.

Printed and bound by CPI Group (UK) Ltd, Croydon, CR0 4YY
Papers used by Scholastic Children's Books are made
from wood grown in sustainable forests.

3 5 7 9 10 8 6 4

www.scholastic.co.uk

1

"Hey, wait for me!" called Sarah, pedalling her bike fast to catch up with her dad and big sister, Zoe. It was a beautiful spring day and Sarah had been distracted by the young lambs in the fields and the

flowers on the verges. Bright sunlight streamed through the trees, making her blink as she approached the others. They had stopped by a gate and Dad was leaning against it, pretending to be asleep.

"I wasn't *that* slow," said Sarah as she pulled up. She exchanged a glance with Zoe and both girls reached out to tickle Dad, who opened his eyes and held up his hands in protest.

"Argh, not the four-armed Tickle Monster! Nooooo!" He rode away quickly, with the girls in hot pursuit, laughing. It was their first family bike ride of the year and it felt fantastic to be cycling along the country lanes near their home. Sarah loved her new red bike, with its sparkly mudguards, shiny silver bell and streamers on the handles – a special present from her family for her ninth birthday. Riding it felt like flying!

Both Sarah and her sister enjoyed doing sporting activities with Dad, who always made every expedition fun. Mum was a bit wobbly on a bike, so was happy to have some quiet time at home, where she would be tucked away in her office, writing the next chapter of her new crime novel.

Sarah noticed that Dad was waving his arm up and down ahead. It meant something was coming, so she and Zoe kept to the side of the lane and rode slowly. Very soon, they heard a strange noise that seemed to be getting louder. Suddenly, around a corner, they spied the reason. It was a flock of sheep approaching!

Baaaa, bleated the animals as a farmer moved them along the lane with the help of his two collie dogs. Dad and the girls pulled over on to a grass verge to let the sheep pass. Sarah tried to count them as they went by, but got in a muddle after fifty as they trotted past in a blur of wool.

"Thank you!" said the farmer, giving them a cheery wave as he passed. Sarah

watched him open a gate and shepherd the sheep into the field, with the dogs rounding up any that wanted to stay munching grass on the verge. In a matter of minutes, the sheep were safely on their new grazing ground, and the farmer was leaning on the gate, watching them, with the dogs at his side. Sarah took a picture of the flock on her phone.

"Come on, daydreamer!" called Dad, who had set off on his bike again, with Zoe close behind.

"I'm taking photos for my art project," Sarah called back, hurrying to join her dad and sister. Sarah's teacher, Miss Tate, had asked everyone to take five pictures of spring scenes. The best ones would go up on the noticeboard in the corridor, and Sarah, who loved art, really hoped one of hers would be chosen.

"You've given me an idea," said Dad, as Sarah caught them up. "I think this ride should be more educational."

Zoe and Sarah groaned.

"What happened to Sundays being *fun days*, Dad?" asked Zoe.

"Don't worry," said Dad. "I just wondered if you'd both like to make a little cross-country detour. We could follow the cycle track through the woods. See things we wouldn't spot otherwise."

Sarah was excited. It would give her the chance to test out her bike's gears over bumpy ground.

"Yes, please," she replied enthusiastically.

Zoe was already setting off and beckoned for Sarah to follow. "Come on, sis," she said. "Let's set the pace."

"Watch out for tree roots," Dad called after them.

Just up ahead, a post with a bicycle symbol on it pointed left into the woods. Zoe took the lead, and Sarah followed close behind.

The cycle path curved between trees, rose steeply over banks covered with plants, and dropped away towards a small stream. Twigs snapped under their tyres as they rode, and rooks cawed from the tops of tall ash trees as they passed, surprised by the visitors.

Sarah's teeth chattered together as she cycled after Zoe. Her bike's gears made light work of the uneven ground and Sarah found she was easily able to keep up with her older sister.

Soon they reached a small wooden bridge, and Dad suggested they do a challenge.

"Each of us could make a small boat

out of sticks. We'll put them in the stream, and the first boat to sail under the bridge and appear on the other side will be the winner. We could set a time limit of five minutes. What do you think?" asked Dad.

Sarah thought this would be fun. Zoe, who preferred computer challenges, pulled a face. Both girls dismounted, leaned the bikes against a tree and went in search of sticks. Sarah quickly made a thin twig-boat with a leaf sail. Zoe fashioned a mini canoe out of a branch by peeling back the bark to create pointed ends. Dad made a small, flat raft, held together with reeds that he tied in an artistic knot. When each boat was ready, Dad and the girls crouched by the edge of the stream, holding them above the shallow water.

"Ready?" said Dad. "Get set. Go!"

The boats dropped into the stream, which was moving slowly, bubbling and babbling over stones. Dad's raft sank immediately and he put his head in his hands in pretend shame. Zoe's canoe was heading for the bridge, carried by the gentle current. Sarah's boat grounded for a moment on a reed, then seemed to spin round and sail backwards, catching up with the canoe.

"Come on!" urged Sarah, clapping her hands.

The girls ran on to the bridge, where they cheered their makeshift boats as they disappeared underneath. Seconds later, it was Sarah's boat that appeared, minus its sail, on the other side.

"The winner!" Dad announced. "Well done, you two. Your boats went much further than mine."

"Girl power," said Zoe, giving Sarah a high five. "So, what's the next challenge, Dad?"

"That's easy. We're going to play our favourite travelling game. Can you guess?" he replied, setting off on his bike again.

"I Spy, yay!" said Sarah, who loved word games. "Do you want to go first, Dad?" she asked.

Dad looked pleased. He started to look around for inspiration as they rode along.

"Hmm. I spy with my little eye, something beginning with B." Dad's face didn't give away any clues. He wasn't staring at anything in particular.

"Branch?" suggested Zoe.

"Nope," replied Dad.

"Bee?" Zoe pointed to a large bumble bee, buzzing near Dad's head.

"Where?" asked Dad, crouching low over his handlebars and pretending to be scared. "Not correct, by the way."

"Is it a badger sett?" said Sarah as they passed a large entrance hole in a grassy mound to their left.

"Right answer, eagle eyes. How did you know that?" asked Dad.

"The hole looks like a letter D lying on its side," Sarah answered without hesitation.

"Nature nut," said Zoe, smiling at her sister. "All those animal magazines you read are turning you into a real expert."

"That explains it," said Dad, impressed. "Do you think the badgers are watching us?" he said, looking around suspiciously. "They might be hiding in the trees."

"Badgers don't climb trees," giggled Sarah. "And they're nocturnal, so they'll be asleep during the daytime."

Dad put his finger to his mouth. "Let's be very quiet then," he whispered.

The cycle track was widening, and in a few moments it opened back on to the country lane. Now they were riding on smooth tarmac again, and Sarah felt her arms relax their hold a little. They were a bit stiff after gripping so hard. But it had been worth it. Riding through the woods had been a real adventure, and her confidence on her new bike was growing by the minute.

"Your turn," Zoe reminded her. Sarah was still thinking about the badgers and had almost forgotten the game!

"Let me see.' Sarah looked from side to side and then up the lane, where there was a small lay-by ahead. "Um . . . I spy with my little eye, something beginning with . . . oh my goodness!"

"'Oh my goodness' isn't a letter, silly," said Dad.

But Sarah was applying her brakes and scuffing her feet along the lane to slow herself down. She stopped her bike in the lay-by, propped it against a hedge and knelt by a grassy verge.

Dad and Zoe followed and were soon watching Sarah reach down and try to lift a cardboard box. The box was covered with a lid, which had been sealed shut with thick tape.

"Well spotted, Sarah. I think you're a bit of a detective, like Inspector Wilding in Mum's books," said Dad. "It's good to clear up litter. We can pop it in the recycling when we get home."

"No, Dad. It's not empty. There's something inside. And it's heavy, too." Sarah was having difficulty picking it up.

Dad bent forward and held the box so that Sarah could unstick the tape and remove the lid. As she did so, she let out a surprised gasp. Dad's eyebrows furrowed in disbelief and Zoe's mouth opened in a silent *Oh*.

The sight that greeted them was something so unexpected, they were lost for words. Out of the box popped a pair of long black fluffy ears, followed by a black and white furry face, bright eyes and twitching whiskers. The face looked at each of them in turn, then disappeared again nervously. Sarah peered inside the box, astonished to see a small creature trying to hunch down and hide itself.

"It's a bunny!" she exclaimed quietly, eyes wide with amazement.

2

"What are you doing out here all on your own?" said Sarah to the small rabbit. "Poor little thing." She tried to tempt the rabbit to eat some grass, but it just twitched its nose and blinked at her.

"What shall we do, Dad?" Sarah felt an equal mixture of concern and surprise at their discovery.

Dad was looking at the rabbit closely. "Well, we need to get Bunny checked over properly." He picked up the box's lid, examined it and shook his head. "No wonder you're a bit thin," he said to the

rabbit. “How long have you been here by the roadside, eh?”

“If only Bunny could talk and tell us what happened,” said Sarah. “I’m sorry you’ve been stuck in a box,” she told the rabbit. “We’re going to help you and everything will be OK,” she added.

“You’re very pretty, aren’t you?” said Zoe to the small creature. “I love the black patches on your face and paws."

Sarah nodded in agreement. "You could be someone's pet, couldn't you? And now you're all lonely and scared. I wonder if you're thirsty."

Dad took the water bottle from the rucksack and poured a capful. He gave it to Sarah, taking care not to spill any.

"Here you are, Bunny," she said, putting it in the box. The rabbit sniffed it, and then Sarah saw a small pink tongue dart out and take a few laps. "Is that better?" she asked.

"Bunny's probably used to the dark," explained Dad. "We'll put the lid back on for now, in case it's scared or tries to hop off." Dad carefully laid the lid across the box, leaving a gap at one end.

"It must be a bit strange having three people staring at you," Zoe agreed.

Dad ran his hand through his hair, the way he always did when he was deep in thought. "We could take Bunny to a vet, but that would mean carrying the box on the bike. I don't think that's sensible, after everything our little friend's been through. Perhaps there's a rabbit rescue place we can ring," Dad said, taking his phone out of his pocket.

Sarah suddenly had a thought. "There's a helpline you can phone if you find an animal in trouble. I've seen it in the RSPCA magazine," she said.

"That's a great idea, Sarah," said Dad, peering at the phone screen. "But, of course, I forgot to bring my reading glasses," he added with a sigh.

Zoe, the technical whizz in the family, came to his aid. She took Dad's phone and her finger tapped the screen. "Got it!

OK . . . this is the website, and here's the helpline number. It's ringing, Dad," she said, giving him back the handset.

At that moment, the bunny's nose appeared in the gap at the top of the box, sniffing the air inquisitively. Sarah stroked it gently. The rabbit seemed to like this and nuzzled her finger for more fuss.

"That's so sweet," Zoe whispered.

Sarah beamed. "I think Bunny knows we're going to help," she said.

Dad was speaking to someone on the phone and was answering questions. The girls listened intently.

"Yes," said Dad, "the rabbit's very bright and alert. There aren't any visible injuries. Water? Yes, we put some in the box. Grass shouldn't be a problem. We're out in the countryside. OK, we'll pick some from the field, not the roadside. Best not to pick Bunny up, I see. Oh, you can send someone? That's great. We're in Warren Lane, just beyond the woods. Yes, we'll wait here. Thank you." Dad ended the call. Sarah and Zoe were waiting eagerly for information.

"They're sending an inspector to help us," Dad told the girls.

"Are they coming straight away?" asked Sarah.

Dad shook his head. "They'll come as soon as they can, but we may have a bit of a wait. In the meantime, maybe you two could pick some fresh grass for Bunny from the field. And we'd better call Mum and let her know what's going on. We'll ask her to bring a shallow dish, so that Bunny can drink more easily."

Zoe helped Sarah over a stile into the field, where long, lush spring grass was growing in abundance. They picked a handful each and returned to the lay-by, where Dad had moved the rabbit's box into the shade.

Sarah put some of the grass into the box, very gently. Dad motioned her to move a little way away.

"The RSPCA said we should try not to disturb the rabbit," he added.

Just then, Sarah spotted Mum driving along the lane towards them.

"Mum's here," Sarah announced, waving at the car.

Mum flashed the headlights to let them know she had seen them, then parked at the entrance to the lay-by. Dad went to greet her and the two of them returned carrying some seat pads from the garden chairs, a bag full of sandwiches and drinks, and a bowl for the bunny.

"I brought a hasty picnic in case there's going to be a long wait," said Mum. "Now then, where's our lucky find?"

"Here," said Sarah quietly, pointing to the box. Mum knelt next to Sarah as she moved the lid back a little.

"Oh, you little sweetie," whispered Mum. "How on earth did you end up here?"

Bunny blinked, its face tilted on one side, and gave a little shiver.

"Are you trembling? I think you might be cold. The box does look quite damp underneath. Zoe, could you pop back to the car and fetch the travel rug, please? We could wrap it around the bottom of the box to help keep Bunny warm."

Zoe nodded, ran to the car and soon returned with the green rug, the one she and Sarah always snuggled under on long journeys. Mum gently lifted the box so that Sarah could put the rug under it.

"There, Bunny," said Sarah. "Now your box might feel cosier."

Mum had poured some water into the little bowl she'd brought, and Sarah placed it in the corner of the box. The rabbit moved towards it with a small hop and began to drink.

"The bowl's much better than a bottle cap, isn't it?" Sarah said in a soothing voice. The bunny blinked at her, as if answering her question.

Mum and Dad spread the seat pads out on the verge and sat down. Zoe, who always found staying still difficult, said she'd prefer to stand and keep a look out for the RSPCA inspector.

Sarah wanted to check on the bunny every few minutes, but Mum said it was best not to startle it. Sarah tried to busy herself by making a daisy chain, but she was thinking about the bunny, and the slender stems kept breaking.

"Muffin, anyone?" asked Mum, knowing that food was usually a good distraction for her children. "They're choccy chip and vanilla."

Sarah took one and held it, her gaze

resting on the bunny's box. "I hope the inspector comes soon," she said.

"Why don't we think of a proper name for Bunny?" suggested Mum, who was good at keeping everyone's spirits up, even in difficult situations. "We could all choose one and you can pick the one you like the most, Sarah."

Sarah smiled and nodded. Then her expression clouded. "But we don't know if Bunny is a girl or a boy."

"Then we'd better come up with names that could work for either," said Dad. "Like Bungle."

"How about Lucky?" Zoe suggested.

"Or Currant Bun?" added Mum.

"They're all good," said Sarah. "But if it's all right with the rest of you, I think we should call the bunny Muffin, because its coat is white with black bits, just like the cakes you've brought, Mum."

"That's a lovely idea." Mum put an arm around Sarah and gave her a gentle squeeze.

"I just hope Muffin will be OK," said Sarah.

"I know, sweetheart, but the inspector will know just what to do," Mum reassured.

"Here comes a van!" Zoe said suddenly. Sure enough, a vehicle was driving along the lane towards them. As it got closer, it was possible to see that the driver was a young woman, in uniform. She drew up close to the family, parked and got out.

"Are you the Mortons?" she asked. "I'm so sorry for the wait. Untangling an escaped sheep from a gorse bush can be a tricky business. I'm Jenny, by the way."

She greeted the family. Sarah noticed the letters RSPCA on Jenny's jacket, and

saw that under the inspector's cap was a blonde fringe and neat ponytail.

After the introductions, Jenny was keen to meet the rabbit.

"This is Muffin," said Sarah, leading Jenny to the box. "We named the bunny just now."

"Hello, Muffin," said Jenny, lifting the lid from the box. "It's nice to meet you. Now, the very first thing we have to do is take your picture. Sarah, can you show me exactly where you found Muffin?" asked Jenny.

Sarah hurried to the spot by the verge where she had first seen the box. Jenny nodded, and then removed the grass and water that had been given to Muffin, replaced the lid on the box and carried it to the exact place, setting it down carefully.

"In cases where animals have been abandoned, we need visual evidence in order to bring a case against the owners," she explained, taking several shots of the box from different angles.

"I'll just take some of Muffin with the lid off," she added. "There. All done. Now let's have a proper look at you, little bunny."

"Would you like me to help?" asked Sarah hopefully.

"That's very kind, Sarah," said Jenny, "but it's best for Muffin to be checked over in the van, without any onlookers. An enclosed space is safer and less frightening for a rabbit. I'll report back in a few minutes, though, I promise."

Sarah watched Jenny carry the box holding Muffin to the back of her van, open both doors wide and lift the box inside. The doors blocked her view after that. She saw Mum and Dad sitting on the verge, deep in conversation. Mum beckoned to her to join them, but Sarah felt anxious and didn't want to sit down. She decided instead to take some photos of her own – of the RSPCA van, of the spot where she had found Muffin, and of her family, waiting for news. It helped to pass the time.

After several minutes, Jenny joined

them and Sarah was relieved to see that she was smiling.

"Well, the first thing I can tell you is that Muffin's a girl," said Jenny. "And I'd say she's about six months old. She doesn't seem to have any injuries, but the vet at the centre will give her a complete examination. In fact, apart from being underweight, she's in surprisingly good shape, despite her recent experience."

Sarah exchanged a relieved smile with her family, who were all very pleased to hear the positive news. Then she looked at Jenny, eyes wide, eagerly hoping for more details.

"You'd like a full report?" Jenny responded. "OK. I checked her eyes, nose and ears, and there's no sign of infection. Her bottom and tail were clean – that's a good sign. Her nails and teeth are normal size for her age. Her coat is in good condition and there are no sores on her paws. I mentioned that her weight needs to increase, and that will be managed over the next few weeks at the centre. Oh, and one last thing," said Jenny. "She was happy to be handled and seems used to people. I think she's a complete star."

"Will you try to find the owners?" Sarah asked.

"Yes. We'll put out an appeal for information, which could take up to three weeks. Abandoning an animal like this is a criminal offence, so if we are able to find the owners, they'll have some explaining to do," said Jenny.

"What will happen to Muffin?" asked Sarah. She could feel something odd fluttering in her stomach – a tiny hope was beginning to form.

"After she makes a full recovery, we'll think about finding a new home for her. In the meantime, a big well done to all of you. Muffin has a second chance thanks to you."

"It's all down to Sarah," said Dad. "She spotted the box, and she suggested calling the RSPCA."

"You should be very proud of yourself." Jenny smiled at Sarah, who felt herself blushing. "Would you like a little look at Muffin before we go?"

Sarah nodded enthusiastically and followed Jenny to the back of the van, where Muffin was sitting in a large animal carrier, munching on some hay.

"Aw. She looks happier already," said Sarah, gazing at the bunny. "Thanks for letting me see her."

Sarah moved nearer to the animal carrier. Muffin watched her and hopped closer, pushing her nose through a gap in the carrier's side.

"I think she wants you to give her a little stroke," said Jenny quietly.

Sarah rubbed Muffin's nose gently with a finger. Once again, the rabbit nuzzled her for more fuss.

"She's taken to you, I think." Jenny smiled warmly.

"We're friends, aren't we?" said Sarah to the rabbit. Muffin blinked and Sarah's face lit up with a smile.

Jenny gently put a hand on Sarah's shoulder. "I need to take Muffin to the centre now."

Sarah nodded a little sadly. "It was really great meeting you, Muffin. You're the nicest bunny ever. I hope someone will take good care of you. Bye bye."

As Jenny closed the van doors, Sarah gave the bunny a little wave and she thought she glimpsed Muffin twitch her whiskers in return.

All too soon, it seemed, Jenny was closing the driver's door and starting the engine. Dad was standing nearby and Sarah took his hand. His grip was firm and reassuring.

Sarah swallowed hard. There was a big

lump in her throat, and tears pricked her eyes.

"Good luck, Muffin," she called, watching and waving until the van, and Muffin, were out of sight.

3

That afternoon, Sarah checked on her fish in the downstairs study. Her mind wandered back to the events of that morning, and as her gaze rested on the black and white pebbles at the bottom

of the tank, Muffin's face seemed to look back at her, rippling in the water. There was movement in front of her eyes, and, when Sarah blinked, she saw her five goldfish gliding in front of her, their beautiful fan tails floating elegantly from side to side. Their mouths opened and closed, as if in silent conversation.

"I hear you," she said. "Dinner time!"

Sarah put just the right amount of flakes in their feeding ring, and the fish swam towards it eagerly. She watched as they fed, enjoying how they interacted with one another.

Sarah had been fascinated by fish since she was a toddler. Whenever anyone asked her what she might be when she grew up, she usually said "a marine biologist", because she loved the idea of learning to dive and studying life in the oceans. But since finding Muffin that morning, she had been considering other possibilities – like training as a vet.

As the sound of the water filter's deep hum lulled her into a daydream, she could see herself working in a surgery, helping all kinds of animals.

Dad appeared in the doorway, snapping Sarah back to reality. "Everything OK in Fish World?" he asked.

"Yup." Sarah nodded.

They had cleaned the tank together before the bike ride. Now Dad cast an eye over the aquarium, making sure everything was still working well. He smiled when he saw the largest of the fish suddenly zip in front of the others, speed through the arch and dive behind the stones. The others quickly followed on its tail.

"I think they're playing chase," said Sarah smiling.

"What's that?" asked Dad, with his hand to his ear. "My *herring's* not too good."

Sarah giggled and repeated her sentence.

"*Cod* you say that again?" Dad teased.

Sarah shook her head and grinned. She loved Dad's funny word games. "Nope. I'm going to *perch* on my bed and read my new magazine. See you later."

She gave him a quick hug before leaving the study, running upstairs to her room and lying down on her bed. She opened her new *Animal Action* magazine and began to turn the pages thoughtfully.

Usually Sarah loved reading the stories and looking at the pictures of baby animals, but today she couldn't focus on the words in front of her. She found the puzzle page and tried to navigate her way through a maze leading to a lost lamb, without success. Then she started a crossword that involved naming different species, but she couldn't even concentrate on that.

She rubbed her eyes and stretched. It had been an exciting day, full of fresh air and adventure. Her mind drifted to thoughts of Muffin once again. It was hard to believe that just a few hours ago, Muffin had been nuzzling her hand. Now it all seemed like a dream.

Next door, Sarah could hear Zoe's favourite band, The Cupcakes, and knew her sister would be sitting at her desk, doing some homework. She loved working with music on. The beat was really funky and Sarah closed her eyes and tapped her feet on the bed in time to the rhythm.

She was just imagining Muffin hopping about to the music when Dad called "Dinner's ready" from downstairs, and her dream world disappeared in an instant.

When the girls arrived in the kitchen, Mum and Dad were serving up a sizzling macaroni cheese bake with garlic dough balls and a crunchy salad. Sarah noticed that their four napkins had been folded in the shape of rabbits, with long ears, and put on their plates.

"Oh, cute. Who did that?" she asked. Mum and Dad both shook their heads, but Dad pointed at Mum behind her back.

Everyone sat down and Mum asked how much bake they would like. Sarah realized that she wasn't very hungry after all, and only wanted a little.

"Aren't you feeling well?" Mum put

her hand on Sarah's forehead to see if she had a temperature.

"I'm fine," answered Sarah. She shook her head when Dad offered her some dough balls. Mum continued to look at her, concerned.

"Do the fish like their new arch?" asked Mum.

"I think so," replied Sarah. "They were zooming through it and around it just now, weren't they, Dad? I might buy them the fairy castle next. They can swim in and out of its windows. And it'll be fun to see them explore. . ."

"But. . .?" Mum could hear the hesitation in her daughter's voice.

"Oh, I was just thinking how nice it was, tickling Muffin's soft furry nose. Fish are lovely, and nice to watch, but you can't stroke them, can you?" Sarah felt her

throat tighten a little as she remembered the morning's events. She stared at her food and pushed it around her plate with her fork, lost in thought.

"She's a very special bunny," agreed Mum. And just think, you helped to save her. If you hadn't spotted her, she might still be by the roadside."

Sarah nodded. Mum was doing her best to cheer her up, but Sarah couldn't help but feel a little hollow inside, knowing she wouldn't see Muffin again.

"Muffin's probably tucking into a bowl of vegetables at this very minute," Zoe added, doing an impression of a bunny eating hungrily.

It seemed to Sarah that her sister and her mum had hatched a plan to stop her feeling sad.

"She'll be eating her favourite food – *bun*-ana custard!" said Dad.

The girls sighed at Dad's bad joke. Mum lifted her eyes to the ceiling.

"I bet she likes broccoli and leafy veggies," said Sarah. "There was a feature about rabbits in my latest *Animal Action* magazine."

"Don't bunnies love carrots most of all?" asked Zoe.

Sarah nodded. "Yes, but they shouldn't eat many, because they're high in sugar.

That's what it said in the article. They're fine as occasional treats, though, but they need to eat hay and grass mostly."

"Sounds like you're a bunny expert," said Zoe, impressed.

"No, not really," replied Sarah. "I've only *read* about owning one. I'd really love to have a bunny of my own one day."

"It's quite a big decision, taking on a rabbit." Mum was thoughtful. "They need special care every day. And one might be lonely on its own, so really it's best to have two, as long as they get on. Furry friends can keep each other company."

That didn't sound so bad, Sarah thought.

"They'd have to have a huge run, wouldn't they?" asked Zoe. "And don't forget you'd have to clean up the zillions of poos they do."

"I wouldn't mind doing all of it," said Sarah quickly. "I'd like to look after them every day."

Zoe put an arm around Sarah. "It's great how much you love animals, sis, but you couldn't take care of them on your own. What about when you're at school?"

Sarah looked at Mum and grinned. "Maybe they could help Mum write her novels!"

"That's a hare-brained scheme if ever I heard it," laughed Mum. "Zoe's right, though. We would all need to be involved."

"And there are other things to consider – visits to the vet, the cost of food and hay. Holiday care," said Dad, doing some quick calculations on a piece of paper.

Zoe chased a dough ball around her plate with her fork. "Maybe Muffin's owners couldn't afford her any more and that's why they left her by the roadside."

"One thing's for sure," said Mum. "Owning rabbits would be a big commitment for all of us." She shared a look with Dad. "Maybe it's something we could think about in the future, when you're a bit older, Sarah."

"Not too much older," pleaded Zoe, "or I might have gone to university!"

Sarah sighed quietly. She was starting to feel a little deflated. There seemed to be so many sensible reasons not to have a rabbit and deep down the small hope she had been nurturing was beginning to fade. Sarah put down her knife and fork. "Sorry, Mum, I can't eat any more. It was really nice though."

"Oh darling, don't be sad about Muffin," said Mum. "The centre will take very good care of her. In fact I have an idea. Why don't I ring the RSPCA tomorrow morning and find out how she is? Would that help?"

"Yeeees!" answered Sarah, her face breaking out into a wide smile. "You could ask if she's eating well, and drinking her water, and hopping about, and twitching her whiskers, and. . ."

Mum smiled. "OK, OK, not too many questions!' she said, holding up a hand to calm her daughter. "You sound like Detective Inspector Wilding."

Sarah clapped her hands excitedly. "You know, I think I might be hungry after all," she said, picking up her knife and fork and tucking into her dinner.

4

"Sarah, have you got ants in your pants or something?" asked Miss Tate at school the next day.

"Sorry, Miss Tate," said Sarah.

Her classmates giggled and Sarah's best friend, Amber, who shared her table, drew an ant with a smiley face on her exercise book.

Sarah looked at it and tried not to laugh. Normally, she was very good at being quiet and concentrating on her lessons, but today she had been tapping her fingers on the table, wriggling on her chair, and looking at the clock on the wall every ten seconds. She felt like an elastic band, stretched tight and ready to snap.

"I'd like you to copy this down, everyone," said Miss Tate, drawing words within circles on the whiteboard.

To Sarah, the words looked like bees buzzing around a flower. Before she realized what her hand was doing, she was drawing a stem, and beneath the stem, a bunny, just like Muffin, nibbling the grass.

"That's very nice, but this is an English lesson, not art," said Miss Tate gently, appearing next to Sarah's desk. Sarah felt her face go hot. The class giggled again.

"Yes, Miss Tate," Sarah responded, staring at the board and hurriedly copying the words.

She had been thinking about Muffin all day long. News of her bunny adventure

had started to spread quickly among her classmates, after Amber had acted out the rescue to a few girls at break time.

They were still talking about it as they returned to their classrooms. Friends had told friends, and those who didn't know Sarah started to call her "the bunny girl".

By lunchtime, even the teachers had heard all about Muffin, and many approached Sarah as she and Amber were eating saying "well done" for helping to rescue the rabbit.

"If you're the bunny girl, shouldn't you be eating veggies?" Amber had teased. Sarah had nodded in agreement, picked up a celery stick from her salad and nibbled it quickly, twitching her nose. It had made them both giggle.

Afternoon lessons had passed in a haze. Muffin was never far from Sarah's thoughts. In PE, the netball coach had told them to jump about to keep warm while they waited for their turn to throw the ball. She had blown her whistle loudly when she realized that Sarah was practising bunny hops.

Bunnies had featured all through the afternoon, too. In cookery, the class had made lemon *buns*, and in art, Miss Tate had asked them to draw a face from memory. Sarah had chosen Muffin as her subject and created a really good likeness.

Sarah sighed. Why was it that the words on the whiteboard looked like rabbits hopping in a line? She rubbed her eyes and checked the clock. Just a few more minutes. . .

"Remember, everyone, the deadline for our spring photo competition is this week, so make sure you bring your pictures in by Friday," Miss Tate announced. Sarah had already given Miss Tate her entry, including her favourite photo of the farmer and his collie dogs.

"Are you entering?' Sarah asked Amber.

"I don't think so," her friend replied. "I tried taking a photo of some flowers but my finger was stuck in front of them. It looked like a pink slug."

"Pink slugs are OK," said Sarah encouragingly.

"But they're not as nice as. . ."

"Bunnies!" the girls said in unison, laughing. She loved how Amber could read her mind.

Sarah gazed at the clock once more and watched as the long hand ticked towards the twelve. *Any minute now*, Sarah thought to herself. Excitement was building in her stomach, matched by the fast beating of her heart.

A shrill, piercing sound rang out in the corridor. There it was! The end-of-school bell was ringing at last.

As soon as she heard the words, "Off you go, class," from her teacher, Sarah rushed to her peg and grabbed her coat.

"You're in a rush today, Sarah," said Miss Tate.

"Mum was ringing the RSPCA to see how the bunny we rescued is," explained Sarah, excitedly.

"Go on then, you two. Hop it!" said Miss Tate with a grin.

Sarah and Amber hurried out to the playground. Sarah saw Mum by the gate and waved.

"Bye, Amber, see you tomorrow," she said to her friend.

"Nighty night, mind the slugs don't bite," said Amber, grinning.

Mum didn't even have a chance to speak before Sarah was asking about the news from the RSPCA.

"Is Muffin eating and drinking, and has she got toys to play with?" The words came out in a rush.

"Don't I even get a 'hello'?" asked Mum, smiling.

"Sorry, Mum," said Sarah, giving her a big hug. "It's just that I've been thinking about Muffin all day and my brain sort of exploded with questions."

"Well, first of all, they said Muffin's made a good start to her recovery," said Mum, unlocking the car.

"Great!" said Sarah, putting her seat belt on. "What else did they say?"

Mum was checking the traffic before pulling out. Once they were driving along, Mum was able to answer.

"Well, it turns out that Muffin's not too far away. Jenny took her to the centre across town. The woman I spoke to said she's settled in well and has been eating greens and lots of hay. She's drinking well and exploring her run."

Sarah nodded, taking this in. "Has she seen the vet yet? Jenny told me Muffin would have a medical check."

"Yes, she's had a vet check and will be microchipped and vaccinated in a few days. The vet's going to neuter her then, too. I think that's everything they told me. Sounds good, doesn't it?" said Mum.

"Sounds fantastic," said Sarah. "Go, Muffin!"

As they drove towards home, Sarah became quiet, thinking about all the things that had happened to Muffin that day. She wished that there was a way she could help the bunny get better. Suddenly, she sat bolt upright in her seat.

"I *could* help Muffin, too," said Sarah. "I could do some fund-raising for the RSPCA. In *Animal Action* magazine, it says they need donations so that they can look after all the animals in their centres."

"That's a brilliant idea. Perhaps Miss Tate would let you run a stall one break time?" suggested Mum.

Sarah nodded. "I'm sure she would.

What could we sell, do you think?"

Mum considered this for a moment. "How about a bake sale? I could help you make cakes."

"Oh, yum, that would be great." Sarah was imagining all the different flavours of cake they could sell.

"And maybe Amber could help as well?" said Mum. Sarah agreed. She was about to text her best friend and ask her when her fingers paused over the keys.

"I was just thinking," said Sarah. "I only met Muffin yesterday, but she's already changed my life. Everyone at school wants to know her story, and now we're planning a fund-raising event. She's making good things happen without even trying. She's a very special bunny, isn't she?"

"I do believe she is," agreed Mum.

5

Amber was just as excited as Sarah about the bake-sale plan, so both girls spoke to Miss Tate the next morning before lessons began. Their teacher thought it was a lovely idea and promised to check with the headmaster for suitable dates later on in the term. She asked if the event had a name.

A title suddenly popped into Sarah's head. "Muffins for Muffin!" she answered.

"That's very clever," said Miss Tate. "Shall we also have 'RSPCA bake sale' somewhere in the name, so that people will know who the funds are being raised for?"

"Yes, because not everyone will know who Muffin is, will they?" Sarah agreed.

"Would you like me to include something about it in the class newsletter?" Miss Tate asked. "Once we have a date, we could ask for cake donations from the rest of the class."

Sarah and Amber both nodded enthusiastically. "The more cakes we can sell, the more money we'll raise," said Sarah.

"We want a cake mountain," exclaimed Amber. "As high as the sky."

News about Muffins for Muffin spread quickly and caused a flurry of excitement. "The Bunny Girl's doing a bake sale," children were telling each other. Even the headmaster, Mr Tilbury, congratulated

Sarah on finding Muffin and deciding to help the charity that had come to her rescue.

"I can see how this encounter has fired you up to help the RSPCA. I've given your bake sale my full support. Well done for getting it off the ground and good luck with the arrangements. Oh, and by the way," he added quietly, "could I put in an order for fifteen cupcakes for the staff room on the day?"

"Of course," said Sarah, writing this down in her notebook.

"That will be seven pounds fifty," added Amber with a cheeky smile.

"You can have it in advance, to help pay for ingredients," confirmed Mr Tilbury.

Amber was doing a little dance on the spot. "We've launched our bake sale," she

said. "You're amazing," she added, giving Sarah a bear hug.

"Muffin's the amazing one," Sarah replied, shaking her head. 'If I hadn't met her, none of this would be happening."

True to her word, Miss Tate included a notice about the bake sale in Form Four's newsletter, which was sent home with each pupil at the end of the week. The date was set for the end of June, in eight weeks' time, and very soon, messages started arriving with offers of cakes for the event.

To Sarah, eight weeks sounded a lifetime away, but with her weekends full of cycling trips, looking after her fish and talking to Amber about plans for the stall, she found that time was passing quickly. Despite all her activities, Muffin was constantly on her mind.

Many times during the day, she wondered how the bunny was getting on at the centre. Just before Sarah closed her eyes at night, she would look at the drawing of Muffin she had brought home from school and imagine what she was doing. She would also tell the bunny how many cakes had been promised for the stall.

"Twenty, thanks to you," said Sarah, blowing the drawing a kiss.

Mum, Dad and Zoe were really

supportive of the fund-raising project. Mum started to make a list of ingredients they would need. Her crime-writers' group offered to lend cake stands and plates, and Dad's law firm donated seventy pounds to the cause. Zoe and her computer-club friends designed posters for the event which Sarah and Amber put up in school.

Two weeks before the bake sale, Mr Tilbury made an announcement in front of the whole school about Sarah's rabbit rescue and decision to organize a fund-raiser. He also referred to Sarah as "a shining example of a pupil who supports animal welfare". He asked everyone to remember to bring a little money to buy a cake on the day.

At home that evening, Sarah was telling her family all about the headmaster's speech when she noticed Mum exchanging a look with Dad.

"I have some news for you, too," said Mum with a smile. "About Muffin."

"What, what, WHAT. . .?" Sarah's eyes were suddenly wide.

Dad held up a hand to try and calm his youngest daughter down. "Mum phoned the centre for an update."

"And?" said Sarah.

"It's really good news," confirmed Mum. "Muffin is back to the right weight. They're very pleased with the recovery she's made. And there's something else. . ."

"Yes?" said Sarah, on the edge of her seat.

"Muffin's made a special friend. He's a rabbit called Monty and he's a year old." Mum smiled as Sarah did a little dance around the kitchen table.

"Muffin and Monty, yay!'" said Sarah, slightly out of breath.

"Apparently they've been living next door to each other for the last couple of weeks and have been getting on really well. In the last few days, they've been given the chance to play together in an enclosure for short periods, so that the staff at the centre could see how they bond," Mum added.

"Don't rabbits mate if they spend time together?" asked Zoe.

"Both Muffin and Monty have been neutered, so it's not a problem," explained Mum. "Apparently, the bonding process has gone extremely well, and now the bunnies are living together happily."

"Aw, that's lovely for Muffin, isn't it?" Sarah sighed. She was so happy that the bunny had made a friend, but a little sad at the same time. She wished more than anything she could see Muffin again, now that she was completely better, and meet Monty, too.

"Did they ever find the owners?" asked Zoe.

Mum shook her head. "Maybe they moved away. Or didn't want to come forward."

"That's not quite *all* the news," said Dad. "There's more." Was that a twinkle in his eye Sarah could detect?

"And it'll affect all of us," said Mum, nodding, a smile playing around her lips.

Sarah looked at Zoe, who shrugged. Her big sister was definitely trying not to grin.

"The RSPCA thinks Muffin is ready to be rehomed," said Mum.

Sarah thought she could hear a whole

drum orchestra beating in her chest.

"We've all been talking," Dad continued, "and we've decided that there's a young lady not too far from here who has proved that she's grown-up enough and caring enough to be the best rabbit owner this side of Rabbitsville – with a little help, of course." Mum, Dad and Zoe were beaming like Cheshire cats.

"Me?" said Sarah, in an amazed whisper.

"We've filled in an adoption form online and spoken to the centre, so we hope so," said Mum, giving Sarah a huge hug.

"We've been doing some secret research," said Zoe, putting three rabbit care books on the table. "We wanted it to be a surprise."

"Muffin's going to come and live with us?" said Sarah, not quite believing what she was saying.

Dad was nodding. "As long as the staff at the centre agree. And it won't just be Muffin."

"Monty, too," confirmed Zoe.

For the first time in her life, Sarah thought she might actually burst with happiness.

"What about all the things we'll need?" she asked. "A shelter, a run, food. . ." The words tumbled out in a rush.

"We've made notes from the books and Zoe's been doing research online, too," said Mum. "We'll need to go through our application with staff at the centre so they can be sure that Muffin and Monty are going to the right home. They've invited us all there tomorrow to sort out the paperwork and arrange a home visit from one of their volunteers."

"You'll be able to see Muffin again, and meet Monty," added Dad, speaking slowly, because Sarah was having trouble taking the words in.

She was almost speechless. It was as if her wishes were coming true. "Thank you," she managed to say. "This has just turned into the best day of my life."

That night, as Sarah lay in bed, wide-eyed with excitement, she tried to imagine what it would be like to visit

Muffin. Moonlight shone through her curtains and, for a moment, seemed to make bunny-ear shadows on her wall. Before closing her eyes, Sarah placed the drawing of Muffin next to her on her pillow.

"See you tomorrow, Muffin," she whispered, before giving the drawing a kiss.

6

Sarah dreamed about Muffin and woke up early, when the birds started to sing. The rest of the household were still sleeping, so she read her animal magazines until six-thirty and then popped downstairs to see her fish.

"Guess where I'm going today?" she whispered, eager to tell someone about the exciting event to come. The fish opened and closed their mouths, as if responding.

"To see Muffin and Monty!" said Sarah.

"I think I'm imagining things," said

Dad from the doorway of the study. He was wearing his dressing gown and his hair was sticking up at funny angles. "What happened to the sleepyhead who likes her hot choc in bed at the weekends?"

"I've been awake for hours," replied Sarah. "All I can think about is the bunnies. What time can we go to the centre?"

"Ten o'clock, I think," Dad said, as he picked up the newspaper from the mat in the hall.

Sarah made a face. "That's a whole three and a half hours away," she said.

"Maybe you could go on the RSPCA website and double-check we've included everything we need for the rabbits on our list?" suggested Dad.

"OK," Sarah said, zooming upstairs and

back to her room. Soon, she was so busy reading all the information about rabbits on the charity's site, she almost forgot about breakfast altogether!

At nine-thirty Sarah was ready and waiting by the car.

"*Pleeease* can we go now?" she called.

"Hold your horses. Or should that be bunnies?" said Dad, while everyone got in and fastened their seat belts.

The rescue centre was on the other

side of town and it took twenty minutes to reach, driving through the weekend traffic. The journey passed in a blur for Sarah. Shop windows full of bright displays and busy streets full of pedestrians seemed like splashes of colour without detail. Her mind was imagining one scene only – the moment when she would see Muffin again.

"Here we are," said Dad at last.

They were pulling into a car park next to a large building. Sarah spotted two vans, with RSPCA in big letters on the side panels, parked near the entrance. Jenny was standing next to one of them, talking to a male colleague. She waved when she saw the family. Dad parked in a bay and everyone got out.

"Hello again," said Jenny as they approached. "This is a nice surprise.

Are you visiting the centre today?"

Sarah nodded eagerly. "We might be adopting Muffin, and Muffin's friend, Monty," she told the inspector.

"That's wonderful!" responded Jenny. "You must be very excited."

"This much!" said Sarah, holding her arms out wide.

Jenny smiled. "I'll take you to reception straight away then," she said. "One of the animal care team will be able to show you around."

Sarah grinned and grabbed hold of Zoe's arm as they followed Jenny into the centre.

The reception area was bright and cheerful, with framed pictures of animals on the walls. Jenny introduced Natasha, the supervisor in charge of the small animals at the centre. Sarah liked Natasha straight away, not least because she wore a pretty paw-print headband in her curly black hair.

Jenny then wished the family well and said she hoped their adoption would be successful. With her bleeper going off, she waved a hasty farewell and left the centre.

Sarah was soon listening to Natasha explain how the charity tried to match pets with the best possible owners. There were lots of factors to consider, including lifestyle, income, time available and experience with animals. The answers the family had given online would be very important in helping Natasha decide their ideal pet or pets, she said.

Sarah pointed out that she already knew who her ideal pets were – Muffin and Monty!

Having gone through their online

application, Natasha said they could visit the rabbits. Sarah's face lit up with anticipation. Natasha asked the family to follow her. She led the way down a corridor, past a number of doorways. Sarah glimpsed inside the open ones and saw one of the RSPCA team examining a cat on a table. Another room looked like a pharmacy, with shelves full of bottles, small boxes and dressings.

Moments later, they were crossing to another building through a glass-covered walkway. They passed a large open-plan area where there were several tall enclosures with large runs attached. Sarah spotted some small furry creatures with big eyes. They looked rather like squirrels. She paused to look at them more closely.

"Those are our chinchillas," said Natasha. "One of our inspectors rescued

four of them recently. The elderly owner couldn't care for them properly, so signed them over and asked us to rehome them. We do get some unusual residents from time to time."

"Do you take in wild animals, too?" asked Sarah.

"Not at this centre," answered Natasha. "Here we focus on adoptions and rehoming, as well as microchipping, neutering and offering advice. As you might have seen, cats and dogs are looked after over there on the western side of the site. And here on the eastern side . . ." said Natasha, holding open a glass door that led to a secure, outdoor area, ". . . we have our rabbits that are ready for rehoming."

Sarah's eyes lit up at the sight of several rabbit houses, raised off the ground. The houses were built out of bricks and each had a large indoor space and a shelter, connected to big outside runs. The runs contained digging boxes full of sand and Sarah could also see some rabbit-friendly toys, including willow balls and cardboard tubes filled with hay.

"We have ten lovely bunnies in this area at the moment," said Natasha. "And, as I mentioned on the phone, where possible, we keep them in friendly neutered pairs for company. So, Sarah, can you spot Muffin?"

Sarah gazed at each run in turn. In the first, a large, jet-black rabbit was munching hay, and its partner – which was grey and white – was sitting nearby with its eyes closed. The second run seemed empty, but Natasha pointed to a dark brown furry nose peeking out from the entrance to the sleeping area.

Natasha explained that rabbits were most active at dawn and dusk, so often preferred to stay in their sleeping areas around noon. But, as Sarah could see, they had access to their runs at all times.

Sarah listened intently, but her eyes were searching all the runs for one familiar furry face.

Natasha had walked to the third run and was motioning for Sarah to come close. "Have a peek," she said quietly, pointing to a large play tunnel made from a wide plastic tube. Sarah knelt down and peered through the mesh of the run.

When she saw what was inside the tunnel, her hand went to her mouth and she gave a small gasp of pleasure.

"It's Muffin!' she said. "She looks so much bigger."

Natasha nodded. "Muffin's now the right size for a six-month-old rabbit. She's been on a special diet of extra nutrients to get her fit and well. Now she eats the same as Monty – lots of hay, a handful of green veggies, a small portion of rabbit pellets and an occasional slice of apple or carrot as a treat."

"Hello, Muffin! Do you remember me?" Sarah gazed at the bunny fondly. Muffin hopped towards her and sniffed at the mesh between them.

"I think she does remember you," said Natasha. "Rabbits are intelligent animals."

"I can't see Monty." Sarah was searching the run for signs of Muffin's new friend.

"He's never far away – they're inseparable." Natasha looked at the other end of the tunnel and smiled.

Sure enough, Monty was there. He

scurried out of the end of the tube and moved close to Muffin, so that his brown coat was touching hers. Sarah noticed straight away that he was larger than Muffin, with white tips on his paws and his tail.

"Oh, look at that!" said Sarah as Muffin began to lick his head.

"She's grooming him. That shows what good friends they are," said Natasha.

"Look, he's closed his eyes – definitely chilling out," said Zoe.

Natasha nodded. "He is, but don't be fooled. He can be very cheeky, too. When you offer him some broccoli to nibble from your hand, he's likely to snatch it and eat the lot!"

Hearing this, Monty pricked up his ears. Everyone laughed.

"I must say," said Dad, "it would be nice to have another male about the place. Boys should stick together, eh, Monty?"

"Hey!" said Mum and Zoe together in protest.

Sarah couldn't take her eyes off the rabbits. It was hard to believe that soon they could be coming home to live with her.

"Feel free to stay with the rabbits for a

while," said Natasha. "My colleague, John, is just over there. He can help you if you have more questions. When you're ready, ask for me at reception and we'll make an appointment for a home visit from one of the team." Seeing Sarah's worried face, she added, "It's nothing to worry about. We always come and check that everything is ready and suitable for the rabbits – secure shelter with a big run attached, the correct food, no dangerous plants in the garden, that kind of thing. It's just to make sure our adopters are prepared and our animals are going to be really happy in their new homes."

Sarah asked if there was a checklist of items they could take away and Natasha confirmed that an information pack was waiting for them at reception.

"Thanks so much, Natasha," said Mum,

shaking her hand. "We're really grateful for all you and your team have done for Muffin. And Monty, too."

Natasha smiled. "I'm so glad that everything worked out, and that hopefully both these bunnies will have a lovely new home. In this case, it seems absolutely right that the little girl who found Muffin should be her new owner. Sorry I've got to dash off – Saturdays are always hectic here!"

"Don't worry at all," said Mum. "You've made one little girl very happy indeed." Mum pointed to her younger daughter, who seemed glued to the ground, watching Muffin and Monty.

Sarah didn't notice Natasha giving the family a wave before walking back towards reception. She was too busy enjoying the sight of both bunnies digging in the sandbox together. She would gladly have spent all day with them, but eventually Mum said it was time to go home. Natasha's colleague, John, promised he would tell Sarah some "fascinating rabbit facts" on the way back to reception to make the parting a little easier.

"Muffin, Monty, I've got to go now," said Sarah. "But we might be coming to collect you very soon, and then you'll have a huge, fantastic, wonderful new adventure."

She used her mobile phone to take a photo of the bunnies and then joined her family, who were waiting with John by the glass door. He started to take them to reception. Sarah was looking back over her shoulder. Her eyes lingered on Muffin and Monty. She gave them a little wave and thought she saw Muffin twitch her silky ears back at her.

"I'm glad they've got all that space to play in," said Sarah.

"They need lots of room so they can run around and even stand up," explained John. "In the wild, they'd live in an area the size of thirty tennis courts."

Sarah gulped. "Oh my goodness! In that case, we're going to need the biggest run ever!"

7

The next week was one of the busiest Sarah could remember. At home, there was a flurry of activity in preparation for the new arrivals.

After reading all the information from the RSPCA about rabbit care, the whole family set to work. Sarah checked the list Natasha had given them and added extra items they could buy or make, including bunny toys. Mum started to weed the garden, removing any plants that could be poisonous, like ivy or rhubarb. Dad and Zoe checked all the fencing and blocked up any holes so that the rabbits would sometimes be able to run free, when Mum and Dad were able to supervise.

By midweek, Dad had set paving slabs on the sand where the rabbit's shelter would be, and laid a wire floor underneath the grassy area where the enclosure would stand. He explained that this would stop the bunnies from digging their way out, and any predators, like foxes, from digging their way in. Sarah had turned two cardboard boxes into rabbit-sized hiding places and was busy painting "Muffin" and "Monty" over the doors.

One evening, Dad went shopping for DIY supplies and then disappeared into the garage, insisting that "no one must come in".

"What's he up to?" Sarah asked Mum.

"Something to do with mending a ladder, I think," answered Mum vaguely, scratching the end of her nose with a muddy finger.

Sounds of power tools and lots of banging echoed from the garage. When Dad emerged, he was covered in pale yellow shavings and smelled of wood.

"I've arranged to take the rest of the week off. My project is going to take much longer than I thought," he said with a wink.

"What project?" asked Sarah as they walked to the kitchen.

'Ah, all will be revealed," replied Dad, a little mysteriously.

"Can I take a peek?" Sarah was keen to see what he was working on.

"Not yet. It's not good to breathe all that dust. The garage is out of bounds for now." Dad helped himself to a biscuit, then returned to the garage, closing the door behind him.

Sarah's mind was busy with bunny thoughts, and so Dad's rather unusual behaviour didn't trouble her. She joined Mum and Zoe in the garden, where Mum was mowing the lawn and Zoe was putting the cuttings in a black plastic bin liner. Sarah noticed that the area set aside for the rabbits had been left uncut. The grass there was long and lush, and dotted with dandelions.

"It's looking really nice," said Sarah. "Can I help?"

"You can rake the grass if you like – make sure there are no loose cuttings left behind," said Mum. "They're bad for bunny tummies."

Soon, the whole area was looking neat, tended and rabbit-friendly, and Mum, Sarah and Zoe had rosy cheeks from the exercise.

"I think we deserve a nice cold drink now," said Mum. "Let's go inside and you can both help me decide what we have for supper."

Bang, bang, bang, went Dad, in the

garage. The girls exchanged a quizzical glance before following Mum to the kitchen.

"How's your bunny list coming along?" asked Mum while making milkshakes.

"Really well," replied Sarah. "Shall I read it to you?"

"Yes, please," said Mum as she whisked chocolate powder into a jug of milk.

"OK," said Sarah. "Rabbit house. Run. Water bowls. Food balls. Hay for food and bedding. Platforms. Digging box and sand. Play tunnels. Pellets. And toys."

"That sounds great, Sarah. I think you've remembered everything," said Mum. "We can pop to the pet shop after school tomorrow. Dad thinks we should get the rabbits' house and run from the garden centre, as there's a really big selection there, so we could do that at the weekend, couldn't we? Then the home checker from the RSPCA will visit next Monday evening, and, if everything's OK, very soon. . ."

"We'll pick up Muffin and Monty!" finished Sarah happily.

At last, the end of the week had arrived. Just before the bell, during the Show and Tell session, Miss Tate asked Sarah to update the class on her adoption application. Sarah told everyone about all the preparations that had been going on at home. She showed them the latest picture of Muffin and Monty on her phone. The children gathered round to look and were very happy to hear that Muffin had found a friend, and that, hopefully, both bunnies would soon be living with Sarah's family. Sarah spoke with new confidence, and Miss Tate complimented her on her talk.

"Close your eyes. Don't peek," said Amber as the class tidied their desks, ready for going home time. She placed something very light, wrapped in pretty pink paper, in Sarah's cupped hands.

"You can look now," said Amber.

Sarah opened her eyes, and was touched to discover the surprise was a page of bunny stickers.

"I thought you could put them on their house or something," added Amber.

"I will. They're brilliant, thanks." Sarah gave her friend a hug. "And as soon as the bunnies have settled in, Mum said you can come for tea and meet them."

"I wanna, I wanna, I wanna . . . yeah!" replied Amber, doing her favourite dance in response. Sarah laughed. Amber had a funny way of reacting to invitations!

The bell sounded, and soon Sarah was running to meet Mum. Finally, they were on their way to the pet shop! Mum had brought the list and Sarah added two more things to it.

"What have you written?" asked Mum, starting the car and driving towards town.

"Water plants. And a fairy castle. I don't want the fish to feel left out," replied Sarah.

There was a parking space in the high street, very near the shop, so a few moments later, Sarah and Mum were looking in the window of Perfect Pets at a display of hamster cages, dog leads, and ceramic dishes decorated with cartoon animals.

Sarah loved visiting the shop. Inside, it smelled of sweet hay and animal feed. As it was a specialist centre for fish, one

entire wall was filled with lit tanks full of exotic varieties. She gazed at them all: stripy angelfish, orange and black barbs, silver and red tetras, yellow rainbow fish. . . There must have been more than twenty types. They all looked beautiful in their underwater worlds.

"Hello again, young lady," said the man behind the glass counter, recognizing Sarah and Mum.

In the corner of the shop, a large

shaggy dog was curled up in a basket, wagging its tail. Sarah smiled.

"What's the dog's name?" she asked the man.

"Oh, that's Fergus. He comes to work with me sometimes," answered the man.

"Can I stroke him?" asked Sarah.

"Yes, he's a gentle boy," replied the man.

Sarah bent down to pat the dog, who wagged his tail even harder and rolled on to his back. "Aw, he's lovely," she said.

"He's not for sale, I'm afraid," said the man.

"That's OK. We've come to buy some things for rabbits." Sarah gave Fergus a final scratch on his belly. "There's quite a long list."

"Fire away then," said the man.

As Sarah read out the items, he put

them on the counter and soon it was completely full up. There were so many things that the owner gave Sarah two water plants for the fish for free and only charged half price for the fairy castle.

The shopping trip had been very successful. Now all the bunnies needed was a special house of their own, with a big run attached. Sarah looked forward to visiting the garden centre and choosing one.

When Mum and Sarah returned home, they saw that Dad was still shut in the garage, making a lot of noise with his drill.

"Do you think he'd like to see what we've bought?" asked Sarah, longing to show Dad and her sister everything in the two big carrier bags.

"Maybe we should wait until dinner,"

said Mum, pointing to the "No Entry" sign that had appeared on the garage door.

When Zoe arrived home from computer club on her bike, Sarah proceeded to tell her all about the trip to the pet shop. Then Mum announced that she needed to pop out for a moment. She asked the girls to lay the table and told them she wouldn't be long.

"Please don't look out of the window for a while," said Mum as she went out of the back door to the garden.

"What's she up to?" said Zoe suspiciously. "Mum and Dad are behaving a bit weirdly, aren't they?"

Sarah agreed. "Have you seen the sign on the garage door?" she asked her sister. "Something is definitely going on."

Just at that moment, there was a loud banging on the kitchen window. The girls jumped. Dad was beckoning them outside.

They hurried to join him. Dad led them across the garden to where Mum was waiting in the rabbits' new area. She was standing next to a very large object, which was covered in a sheet. She and Dad exchanged a look, picked up the ends of the sheet, shook them upwards, and Dad said "Ta-da" in a loud voice.

As the sheet billowed upwards, like a sail catching the wind, it revealed a building

underneath. When she saw it, Sarah let out a gasp of delight, as the building was a small wooden bungalow, raised from the ground on a base. It had a grey painted roof with a small chimney, two windows and a bunny-sized door, from which a ramp sloped gently to the ground.

"Dad, did you make this? It's AMAZING!!" exclaimed Sarah. She gazed at Dad's creation, trying to take in every single detail. Attached to the bungalow was a large enclosed run, probably three metres long and almost as tall as Sarah herself. The run was made of wood and mesh, and there was a gate on one side for access. There was enough space for Muffin and Monty to stand on their back legs, if they wanted to, and to run and hop as much as they pleased.

"This is the coolest bunny house I've

ever seen," agreed Zoe, who had lifted off the roof of the house to reveal spacious living accommodation.

Dad smiled. "You know, I'd forgotten how much I enjoyed woodwork," he said.

"It's going to be the Bunny Bungalow," said Sarah, peeking through the windows. "Muffin and Monty will love it. Thanks so much, Dad," she added, giving him a tight squeeze that made sawdust fall from his shirt.

With the special shelter and run in place, Sarah and her sister decided where the recently bought bunny items should go. Sarah enjoyed going in and out of the run on her hands and knees, putting toys in position. Mum and Dad laughed when Sarah and Zoe pretended to be bunnies, hopping after one another!

Sarah stood up and checked the

bungalow and run one last time, to make sure they hadn't forgotten anything.

"Wait!" she said suddenly, disappearing inside the house and returning with something in her hand. "Amber's stickers! It wouldn't be the Bunny Bungalow without them."

The RSPCA volunteer, whose name was Sam, arrived on Monday evening, and Sarah and her family waited a little nervously to hear whether they had prepared everything in the right way for the arrival of Muffin and Monty.

Sam checked the rabbits' new home and was very pleased to find that there was plenty of bedding, that their water and food bowls were in place, and that there was a good supply of food for them to eat. He liked Sarah's home-made hiding places and was pleased that there was also a digging box, made from a wide, shallow plant pot, with sand inside.

"This all looks great," said Sam. "And I must admit, I've never seen such a grand rabbit house before. It's a really good design, just right for Muffin and Monty. It will be absolutely fine for you to pick them up next Saturday. They are two very lucky rescue rabbits."

Sarah gave a whoop of pleasure at this news and her family joined in.

"That's just the news we wanted," said Dad. "In fact, it's the icing on the cake!"

8

With everything ready for the rabbits, Sarah and her family could turn their attention to the bake sale. Every day after school that week, Sarah, Zoe and Mum made cakes. Soon, the kitchen resembled a bakery, with plates filled with lemon bars, chocolate brownies, Victoria sandwich cakes and lots of biscuits with different designs and coloured icing on top of them.

Amber and her Mum were in charge of rocky road squares, vanilla buns and marshmallow cupcakes. By Thursday, they had made a total of forty-nine. Amber admitted to eating the fiftieth!

Mum helped Sarah make a lemon sponge, just for Mr Tilbury, and then they iced fifteen cupcakes with different toppings, and covered them in coloured sprinkles, ready for the staff.

Zoe made computer-mouse cakes, covered in grey icing, with raisins for eyes, especially for her computer club.

When Dad came home he said the kitchen looked like a cake shop, with trays filled with delicious sponges and iced cupcakes in cases on every surface. He walked around the room, pretending to carry out an inspection.

"No tasting," said Mum, waving a wooden spoon at him.

"Please?" asked Dad, with his hands clasped together. "I'll pay?"

"In that case," said Sarah, "it's fifty

pence per cake."

Dad felt around in his pocket and produced a handful of change. "Here, have all of this," he said, picking up a chocolate cupcake covered in rich, creamy icing. "Oh, that is so good," he murmured, eating it in big bites and then licking his fingers clean.

"What's under the tea towel?" he asked.

"They're the extra-special cakes," explained Sarah, wiping icing sugar from her nose. She lifted the towel to reveal a plastic box filled with twelve muffins,

topped with white chocolate icing and a marzipan bunny on the top.

"Muffin's muffins," she said with a smile.

The next morning, Mum drove Sarah to school extra early so that they could set up the stall on the table in the main hall, ready for the sale.

Amber arrived a few moments later, holding a tray that was laden with treats. She carefully placed the tray full of goodies on the table. When she saw Sarah's bunny muffins, she let out a shriek of excitement.

"They're *so* sweet," she squealed. "Where did you get the marzipan bunnies?"

"Zoe found them online," replied Sarah. "I think we can charge a bit extra for the muffins, don't you?"

"You betcha," said Amber. "They'll cost

extra bunny money."

Just at that moment, Miss Tate entered the hall and said hello to the girls and Sarah's mum.

"Wow, these cakes look fantastic!" she said. "Which ones did you make?" Sarah and Amber pointed to their creations, and Miss Tate congratulated the girls on their baking skills.

Other pupils began to arrive with cakes for the sale, and soon the table was full of plates, cake stands and the most delicious-smelling delights Sarah had ever seen.

"It looks fantastic – like something out of a magazine," said Mum as she was leaving. "Good luck, you two," she added.

"Thanks, Mum," said Sarah, crossing all her fingers. "See you later."

Miss Tate had excused the girls from

registration and their first lesson so that they could prepare for the sale. When the bell sounded, announcing morning break, Sarah looked at Amber.

"Can you hear that?" she asked.

"What?" asked her friend.

"Kids' feet, running," she replied. "Here they come!"

Suddenly, the door to the hall was thrown open and the whole space seemed to fill up with children, all eager to choose a cake from the stall. A long, winding snake of a queue formed, wriggling and jiggling as the eager tasters waited their turn.

Luckily, Miss Tate was on hand to help take the money and hand out change. In just five minutes, the plastic container was brimming with coins, so the teacher emptied it into a carrier bag.

Mr Tilbury popped by to collect his lemon sponge and the cupcakes for the staff. He was delighted to find that his cake was decorated with a yellow ribbon and thanked Sarah and Amber for their hard work.

Sarah's bunny muffins were very popular and disappeared quickly. One older boy bought three at once and said they were the best muffins he'd ever eaten.

Break time passed in a commotion of chatter, cake choosing and happy chomping. When the bell sounded once more, all that was left on the table was an array of empty plates and an assortment of crumbs.

Miss Tate counted the money quickly.

"How much did we make?" asked Sarah anxiously.

"One hundred and fifty-five pounds," said Miss Tate. "Congratulations, girls!" The teacher beamed. "I think the RSPCA will be very pleased indeed."

Sarah's face relaxed into a wide smile. She gave Amber a high five. "Queens of cake," she announced.

"Yeah," replied Amber with a giggle. "Sponge sisters. Because we're always sandwiched together!"

Sarah decided it was her best Friday ever. The smile that had spread across her face after the bake sale lasted all day, through every lesson, and up to the moment when her teacher announced the winners of the photo competition, just before the last bell.

"I'm delighted to say that everyone who entered from this class has had at least one picture chosen to go on the wall," said Miss Tate. "Congratulations, all of you," she said smiling. "And well done to Sarah, whose photo of a farmer and his dogs received a special mention, and to Amber, whose worm made the judges laugh! I'm awarding you all two effort marks, and please take a chocolate from the box on your way out."

Sarah looked at Amber in surprise.

Amber shrugged and grinned. "I just played around with the picture of my finger on the computer and added a face," she said. 'Not just any old face. Our headmaster, Mr Tilbury!"

Sarah giggled. What a brilliant end to the week! As she and Amber chose a sweet from Miss Tate's box, their teacher asked them to wait a moment, as Mr Tilbury wanted to give them something before they went home.

When Sarah turned round, her head teacher was standing next to her. In his hand was a cheque with "RSPCA" on the top line and "One hundred and fifty-five pounds" written underneath.

"Excellent work, girls," said Mr Tilbury, shaking their hands. "I expect you'd like to give this to the charity in person, Sarah?" He gave her the cheque and wished Sarah and Amber a very happy weekend.

"And good luck with the new additions to your family," added Miss Tate, who remembered that Saturday was going to be a big day for Sarah.

"Thank you," replied Sarah.

"Send me a picture as *sooooon* as the bunnies arrive," pleaded Amber.

"I promise," replied her friend as they hurried towards the gate, where both mums were waiting to collect them.

That evening, after dinner, Sarah popped out into the garden and visited the Bunny Bungalow for the fifth time since coming home from school. It reassured her that the arrival of the rabbits wasn't just a dream, but would soon be a real event.

"This time tomorrow, you'll both be

here," she said, hoping somehow that her words would be carried to Muffin and Monty on the warm evening wind.

And when night fell, and Sarah was about to hop into bed, she looked out of her window at the rabbit house and run, which were bathed in moonlight, and her heart almost skipped a beat. *In just a few hours,* she thought, *there will be bunnies living in my garden*!

9

Early the next morning, the Morton family were travelling towards the RSPCA centre in the car. Zoe and Sarah were chatting animatedly about the bunnies, and how they would settle in.

"Who do you think will be the first to explore the Bunny Bungalow?" asked Sarah.

"Monty, probably," said Zoe. "I think he might be quite nosy."

"Muffin's very brave, though, isn't she?" Sarah smiled, remembering the first time she glimpsed the little bunny in the box.

Before long, they were pulling into the car park at the RSPCA centre. There were several vehicles there already. Sarah wondered if other animals were being collected by families that day. It was nice to think that perhaps more pets were being rehomed and starting a new life, just like Muffin and Monty.

John was waiting for the family at reception. Sarah offered him an envelope containing the cheque for the RSPCA and explained that she and Amber had run a bake sale for the charity. John took out the cheque, looked at the total and gave an impressed whistle.

"That's fantastic," he said. "And I'm very honoured to accept your cheque on behalf of the organization. We'll send it to head office with your details. I know they'd want me to say a great big *thank you*."

"I just wanted to help," said Sarah.

"You certainly have. Look at all the mouths we have to feed! Every penny really does count, you know," said John. "So, now, are you ready to see your bunnies?"

"Yes, please!" Sarah's voice had become a whisper with excitement.

"Perhaps your dad could open up the car?" asked John. "I'll bring Muffin and Monty round the back way, so it's quieter for them. As you can see, the centre's busy with visitors today."

"Good plan," said Dad. "We'll wait for you outside."

Soon, John returned with a large pet carrier. An expression of wonder appeared on Sarah's face the moment she saw Muffin and Monty, side by side in the carrier. They were sitting on fresh hay,

which they were both nibbling. Also inside the carrier was a willow ball and a cardboard tube filled with torn-up newspaper.

"Their favourite toys," explained John. "It's important for them to have familiar things around them to help them settle into new surroundings."

"They look so sweet!" Sarah said. "Look, Zoe. Muffin's nuzzling Monty."

The girls watched the rabbits for a few moments while John checked that the carrier was secure.

"Okey-dokey," he said, lifting it up carefully. "Time for your mini road trip." John placed the carrier gently on to the back seat and put a seat belt around it.

"Two bunnies, ready to go," he said cheerfully. He bent down, looked at the rabbits and added, "Be good, you two."

"I'm sure they will be," said Mum.

"Now, what is it you have to remember at night time?" John asked Sarah.

"Check their water bowls and make sure there's hay in their den. And that their ramp is clear, because they'll want to use their run," she answered.

"Exactly right. Well done. I can see you've done your rabbit homework!" said John approvingly. "But if you have any questions, just. . ." He held his hand to his ear and made the sound of a phone ringing.

Sarah nodded. "We will," she said, getting into the car and taking a peek at the rabbits as she clicked her seat belt in. She was pleased to see that Monty was already munching on the hay.

"One last thing," said John, producing two wooden chew sticks and giving them to Sarah through the open window. "These are their chew toys. Very good for their teeth as well."

"Thanks," Sarah replied, tucking them inside her pocket.

Soon, the Mortons were driving away from the car park. Sarah and Zoe waved to John until he was out of sight. Sarah sighed happily. There was a *munch, munch, munch* coming from beside her, and the air was filled with the smell of sweet hay.

Upon reaching home, Sarah followed Zoe out of the car and waited for Dad to lift out the carrier. She bent down so that she was at the same level as the rabbits.

"Well done, bunnies. That wasn't so bad, was it?" she said, and Muffin turned her ears towards Sarah, listening to her voice.

"Crikey, these two must have grown since we saw them," said Dad, as he carried the rabbits towards the back garden with Sarah at his side.

She opened the door to the rabbit run and helped Dad put the carrier inside. Then she made sure the run door was closed behind her, took a deep breath and released the catch on the carrier.

"Welcome home, Muffin and Monty," she said.

Sarah stepped out of the run, taking care not to startle the bunnies, and secured the door behind her. Her family stood quietly, watching and waiting. Which bunny would emerge first? Monty was sniffing the air outside the carrier inquisitively, and both rabbits' ears were tilted forwards. They definitely seemed curious about their new surroundings.

Sarah knelt down and crouched low, so that she was only a little taller than the bunnies. Muffin looked at her and twitched her nose. The rabbits seemed reluctant to leave the carrier.

"They might be a bit unsure to start with," said Mum. "The RSPCA said that's quite usual."

Sarah was gazing at them, entranced. Then she had an idea. "I know," she said, remembering she had taken some raw broccoli to the centre, in case the bunnies needed something to eat on their journey. She felt in her pocket. Yes, it was still there. Sarah pushed the small piece of vegetable through the wire of the run. Monty spotted this and immediately hopped out of the carrier towards it, picking the broccoli up in his teeth and nibbling it. "Aha!" Sarah exclaimed. "Now

we know you're the greedy one!"

Muffin approached more cautiously, sniffing the green vegetable, but instead of eating it, she turned round nimbly and hopped up the ramp leading into the Bunny Bungalow.

"She likes it!" said Sarah, as Muffin explored the inside of the shelter and reappeared in the entrance, by the top of the ramp. She rubbed her chin against the wooden shelter and then lay down. "She's put her scent on the house. I think that means she's settling in," Sarah commented.

"They both look very happy," agreed Dad. Sarah could see he was pleased that the bunnies had taken to his creation so quickly.

Zoe was watching Monty, who was drinking from a water bowl. "I bet he's thirsty after all that munching."

Monty drank for a few moments, then hopped around the edge of the run, exploring his new home. He investigated the digging tray with interest, but when he saw the play tunnel, he looked left, then right, before running at full speed into it. Sarah and her family burst out laughing at his antics.

When Monty didn't reappear, Muffin hurried down the ramp. Just as she reached the end of the tunnel, Monty shot out and ran up the ramp into the Bunny Bungalow.

"They're having a game!" said Sarah, delighted, as Muffin followed Monty and scuffling could be heard coming from inside their house.

When the bunnies appeared again, Muffin was leading Monty and this time she was the one who ran inside the play tunnel, then on to the platform. Monty pushed the willow ball with his nose and Muffin hopped in the air, turning nearly a full circle. The play continued for a further few minutes, until both rabbits seemed to tire. Sarah poked the two chew sticks John had given her into the run. Muffin

and Monty took one each and settled down to nibble, calmly and contentedly.

"That will make a lovely picture," said Sarah, reaching for her phone. She took several photos and chose the best one to send to Amber. Her friend texted back straight away: Sooooooooo cute!!! ☺☺☺

Sarah wanted to spend every minute she could with the rabbits, but Mum suggested that it was best to leave them to settle in. So, that afternoon, when the bunnies were resting in the Bunny Bungalow, Sarah sat at the table on the decking, reading the latest edition of *Animal Action* magazine. Every so often, she glanced towards them, and thought how lucky she was that they were her very own pets.

Towards the end of the afternoon, Muffin and Monty reappeared from inside their little house.

"They're in the run again, Mum, look!" said Sarah to her mother, through the open kitchen window.

"Looks like they've had a nice rest," said Mum. "They're scampering about, full of beans, aren't they?"

Sarah laughed as she saw Monty hop right over the top of Muffin and run through the play tunnel.

"Can I go and check on them?" asked Sarah.

"Well, I'm just about to serve up dinner, so why don't we visit them after we've eaten?" suggested Mum.

Sarah joined her family inside and they all sat down to eat dinner. Her mind wasn't on the spaghetti bolognese on her plate, but on the bunnies. She ate her food so quickly, she got hiccups.

"Muffin and Monty will still be there when you go back outside," said Mum. "You don't have to gobble everything down."

"I'm excited – *hic* – about seeing them – *hic* – again!" explained Sarah, trying to remember to chew her food slowly.

When dinner was finished, and Sarah's hiccups had finally gone, Dad accompanied her to the Bunny Bungalow and together they checked Muffin and Monty's water bowls, refilled their hay rack and replenished their supply of leafy greens.

It was time to say goodnight to her new pets. Sarah really wished she could camp out, just so that she could watch them feeding and playing under the stars. She had asked Mum and Dad during dinner, but they had both said a firm "No" to her request!

"Have fun! See you in the morning!" She gave them both a little stroke before going back into the house.

That night, when Sarah looked out of her bedroom window, a very special scene met her gaze – the curving shapes of two bunnies, one larger than the other, side by side in the moonlight.

10

Sarah woke at seven the next morning, after a night filled with bunny dreams. She hurriedly put on her dressing gown and furry slippers, and raced down to the kitchen, where Dad was brewing coffee.

"You've become an early bird," he commented. "Would you like a hot chocolate?"

"Not yet, thanks," Sarah replied, smiling at his untidy morning hair. She took a cabbage from the vegetable rack and snapped off two big leaves. "I'm going to give Muffin and Monty a special treat with their breakfast."

Sarah washed and dried the leaves, then smiled at Dad. "Come on then," she said. "The bunnies are waiting."

"The grass might be a bit wet. Do you want your. . .?" Dad was about to say "wellies", but Sarah was already skipping over the dewy grass in her slippers. She didn't notice that they were soaking up the moisture, or that the bottoms of her pyjamas were getting wet, too. She had one purpose – and that was to attend to Muffin and Monty.

"Clever boy!" she said as she approached the rabbits. Monty was up on his hind legs, watching her approach. Muffin was nibbling grass near the digging tray, but as soon as she noticed Sarah, she hurried to the side of the

run. Sarah grinned. The bunnies seemed pleased to see her!

"Good morning, Muffin. Good morning, Monty. How are you today?" Sarah waited for Dad to catch up, then carefully opened the door to the run and put the food on the grass. The bunnies sniffed the fresh vegetables and Monty began to munch a cabbage leaf straight away. Muffin approached Sarah's hand, so she tickled the bunny's nose.

"Monty, don't pinch all the cabbage," said Sarah, noticing that the larger bunny was about to help himself to Muffin's cabbage leaf. Muffin cocked her head on one side, as if she could understand what Sarah was saying, and then hopped over to the leaf and sat on top of it.

"Ha ha. Clever girl!" laughed Sarah.

'Monty's a mischief," said Dad.

"But Muffin isn't letting him get away with too much, is she?" Sarah added with affection.

In a few minutes, she had filled the bunnies' food balls with their daily ration of pellets, refilled their hay rack, added more hay to their sleeping area, and topped up their water bowls.

"You're an excellent 'bunny mummy'," said Dad to Sarah. "Mum and I think you're doing a fantastic job."

"Thanks, Dad," said Sarah, closing the door to the run. She crouched down to face the rabbits. "I'm going to have my breakfast now," she told Muffin and Monty. Monty looked up at her with a quizzical expression and a long piece of cabbage hanging out of his mouth.

"He's a bit of a jester, isn't he?" said Dad, and Sarah agreed.

Sarah and Dad returned to the kitchen, and before long, the whole family was sitting down to breakfast. Every so often, Sarah glanced out of the window, just to keep an eye on the bunnies. Mum and Dad noticed this and smiled.

"I think Muffin and Monty have changed my life," said Sarah. "I love looking after them. I've decided that I'm going to take pictures of them every day."

"Like a photo diary?" asked Zoe.

Sarah nodded. "Yup. Then I can put them all over my room! Like bunny wallpaper."

"I think they've changed all our lives in a really good way," said Mum. "I was stuck on a name for a special character in my book, but this morning, I woke up and knew exactly what he should be called – Mr Monty!"

"I'm planning my next woodwork project," said Dad. "I might never have got round to it without the Bunny Bungalow."

"And I'm going to design a computer game about bunnies," said Zoe. "It'll be a good project to work on at computer club."

"I think we should propose a toast," said Dad, picking up a thick slice from his plate. "To Muffin and Monty."

"Muffin and Monty," said Sarah, Zoe and Mum, clinking their mugs together.

One July evening, when Sarah was about to stick her twenty-eighth photo of the rabbits on her wall, the doorbell rang.

"I'll get it!" she called, hurrying downstairs, her heart thumping with excitement.

She had been looking forward to seeing this visitor very much. In fact, the whole family had gathered in the hallway, ready to greet him. Sarah recognized his familiar shape through the patterned glass and rushed to open the door.

"Hi, John," she said. "The bunnies are expecting you."

"Hello again, Sarah," said John with a warm smile. "I'm looking forward to seeing the little scallywags. How are they settling in?"

"Come and see," answered Sarah, leading John through the house to the back garden with the rest of her family.

"You all look as if you're very happy with your new arrivals," John commented.

"We definitely are," replied Sarah.

John whistled and smiled broadly when he saw the Bunny Bungalow. "Well, this is very impressive!" he said.

Dad gave John a guided tour of the wooden shelter and run. As he was speaking, the rabbits play-chased and finally sat at the bottom of the ramp, twitching their noses.

"I think they're listening," said Sarah.

John bent down near them. "Well, Muffin and Monty," he said. 'I think your new home is fantastic."

Mum appeared, carrying a pretty plate covered with freshly cooked cakes. "These are a little thank you, John, from all of us," she said.

"Muffins!" exclaimed John, laughing. "That's really kind of you."

"And I have a little surprise for you," said John, taking a camera from his pocket. "The RSPCA wants to feature your rescue story in *Animal Action*. The editor asked me to take a photo of you all today to go with the piece. Bunnies included, of course."

Sarah was thrilled with this news and could hardly believe that Muffin, Monty and her very own family would be appearing in her favourite magazine.

"Now, let's set up a nice picture," said John. "Sarah, you kneel down by the bunnies. Zoe, can you go next to her?

Mum and Dad can stand behind. Perfect. The bunnies are looking straight at the camera. Have you been giving them acting lessons? OK, everyone. Big smile!"

With that, John took the photo, remarking that Sarah's smile was the biggest of all. He showed the family the shot on the camera screen. Everyone laughed because Monty had one eye closed and seemed to be winking at Muffin.

Sarah looked at them affectionately. "They're the best bunnies in the world. I'm really glad that other children will be able to read their story."

"Now that's what I call a happy ending," said John.

At that very moment, Muffin and Monty touched noses.

"They're best friends," said Sarah, "And that's the happiest ending of all."

Meet A Real RSPCA Inspector – Maxine Jones

Photo by Joe Murphy

Sarah and Muffin's story is based on a real-life animal rescue. Could you tell us about a similar rescue you were a part of?

Three baby rabbits were left in a cardboard box down an alley in Middlesex. It had been raining heavily and the box had started to fall apart. One of the rabbits escaped from the box, and a member of the public saw it hopping down the alley, so she went to investigate. She took the bunnies home and called the RSPCA, and I was alerted to the situation. Upon arrival, I gave the bunnies an initial examination. They were still young – probably only about five or six weeks – and were bright and alert, though a little underweight. I checked that their eyes and ears were clear and that they were moving OK. Then I placed the bunnies in a basket lined with newspaper and a small amount of hay and drove to the RSPCA Hillingdon clinic, where I signed the bunnies in. There, the vet checked them over and they were then sent to a boarding establishment until they were ready for re-homing. Now they are all happy with new owners.

Why did you want to work for the RSPCA?

I wanted to do a job that would make a difference and help others. I've always loved animals and so being an RSPCA inspector was the perfect fit.

Could you describe what a typical day at work is like?

There are no typical days – each one is different and brings its own unique challenges. This can range from follow-up visits, to trying to catch a swan with a broken wing in a local park. I will work out an order of priority for the visits and then drive to them in my RSPCA van.

What is the best thing about being an inspector?

It's great to do a follow-up visit and see that the pet owner has taken my advice on board and has made a change for the better. I wanted to be an RSPCA inspector to make a difference to animals and on these occasions I really get to see how I've helped.

To find out more about the work the RSPCA do, go to:

www.rspca.org.uk

Some Tips for Looking After Your Rabbits

Make sure your rabbits always have access to fresh, clean drinking water and lots of good-quality hay or growing grass.

Rabbits love to eat leafy greens (cabbage, kale and mint are some of their favourites!), but only feed your rabbits apples and carrots in tiny amounts as occasional treats.

Rabbits need a large, secure shelter where they can rest. This should be permanently attached to a big exercise area where they can run, jump and dig.

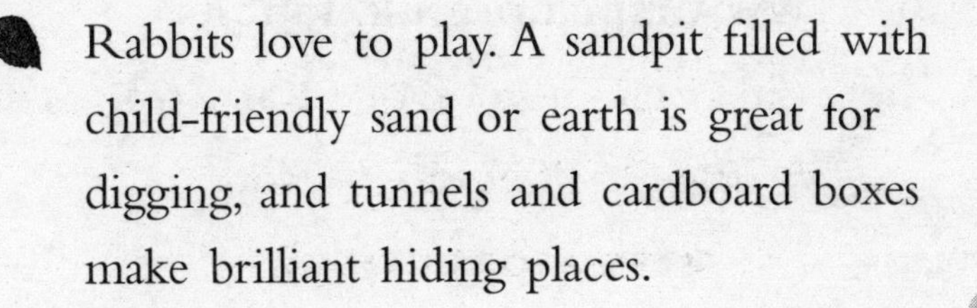

Rabbits love to play. A sandpit filled with child-friendly sand or earth is great for digging, and tunnels and cardboard boxes make brilliant hiding places.

Rabbits need a suitable friend! They are social animals and should be kept with at least one other rabbit in compatible, neutered pairs.

Spend time interacting gently and positively with your rabbits. Sitting with them at ground level, offering healthy treats and allowing your rabbits to come to you will teach them to see humans as friends.

Visit the vet. Regular visits to the vet will keep your bunnies happy and healthy.

For more advice on caring for your rabbits, check out the RSPCA website:

www.rspca.org.uk/rabbits

Facts About Rabbits

- A female rabbit is called a "doe" and a male rabbit is called a "buck".

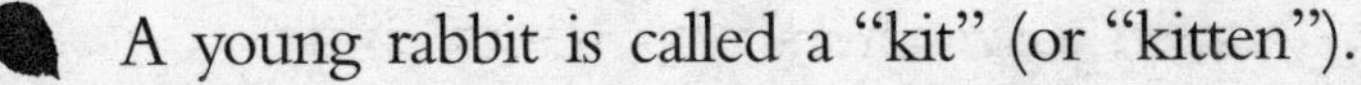

- A young rabbit is called a "kit" (or "kitten").
- Rabbits are herbivores (they only eat plants).

- Wild rabbits live underground, in burrows. A group of burrows is called a "warren" and can house fifty or more rabbits.

- A rabbit's teeth never stop growing.

For more bunny facts, take a look at the RSPCA's rabbit factfile:

www.rspca.org.uk/allaboutanimals/pets/rabbits/factfile